Spunky:
Tapping into Trouble

Sherile Reilly

Produced by:

FriesenPress

Suite 300 – 852 Fort Street
Victoria, BC, Canada V8W 1H8

www.friesenpress.com

Distributed to the trade by The Ingram Book Company

Table of Contents

Dedication & Acknowledgements

For Ed, with love…

Thanks to my friends and colleagues who have helped me so much: Donna Tunney, Suzanne Stengl, Brenda Collins, Diana Scott, Marlene Dunn and Kymber Morgan.

Thanks to my sister, Betty Eileen Bruerton, who has always believed in me and assisted with this novel.

Thanks to Mike Reilly for his computer assistance.

And thanks to two excellent writing groups: The Alberta Romance Writers' Association and the Calgary Association of the Romance Writers of America, better known as ARWA and CARWA.

Chapter One

Tap-tap. Tap-pe-ty-tap. Spunky hopped into the air. When she landed on her tap shoes the sound exploded against the basement cement floor. She grinned to herself as she danced past the washer and dryer. Dancing felt sooo good. It was the first time she'd been able to dance since she'd moved, with her mom, to the main floor of the rented house in Badger Creek.

Keeping her knees bent a little and her hands forward, she pretended that the top of the washer was a stand-up piano. She drummed the rhythm on the metal surface and belted out a song to the beating of the machine. The sharp smell of bleach tickled her nose.

From two windows high above, sunlight shone onto the painted, grey floor like a spotlight on a stage. She tilted her head and her long brown hair swung in front of her eyes. Pulling it back behind her ears, she twisted it into a pony tail, then raised her head and gave a huge smile to her new best friend.

Sitting on the bottom step of the basement stairs, Sammy Wong applauded. "That's great."

BANG!

Across from the laundry room, a door blasted open and an old lady charged out of the basement suite like a stampeding elephant. Then she stopped and glared at Spunky. "What are you doing?"

"I...I was just practicing my dancing," explained Spunky. "Like this." She did a quick shuffle. The taps of her shoes made a fabulous rat-a-tap-tap. After a full turn, she bowed, hoping the old lady would clap or at least smile.

"I was sleeping and you woke me up." The lady scowled. "Noisy little girl. And those..." She pointed to Spunky's black tap shoes. "They make far too much noise."

Spunky glanced down. She'd saved her allowance for the shoes.

"But I don't want to forget the steps. I used to take lessons, you know." Spunky thought about how her dad, when he was alive, had loved to watch her dance. That was before the car crash two years ago. She still missed his big smile and hugs.

When they moved into the rented house last week her mom had told her that a woman, named Mrs. Snodgrass, lived in the basement suite. Maybe if she explained how much she loved dancing, the lady would ask to see her dance steps.

"How old are you?" The woman's nose twitched as if she'd smelled something awful.

"Ten." To Spunky, it was a great age.

"Ten years old. Then you're much too short to ever be a ballerina."

Spunky crossed her arms and stared back. Ballerina? She didn't want to be a ballerina. She wanted to tap dance, so who cared if she was short? She just wanted to sing and dance, and have lots of fun. And most of all, she wanted a new bike so she could ride fast and keep up with Sammy.

"Your movements must be graceful. Like this." The old lady raised her hands and turned her head to the side.

Spunky noticed her sharp, beak nose. Her dress lifted, showing a white slip with lots of lace.

"Ballerinas are slender and tall." Balancing on one foot, she stretched her arms to the side and pointed her fingers, like a windmill. She twirled, reminding Spunky of a spinning top. When Mrs. Snodgrass stopped, she lowered her arms and pointed at the floor. "Mr. Hansen, the landlord, would not be very pleased to have you scuffing the cement. He just painted it."

"My mom never told me..."

"Well now you know." The woman shook her finger. "You, young lady, have a lot to learn. Being as you've just moved in, I'm sure your mother hasn't explained the rules. I hope you both realize how much sound carries." The old lady tightened her lips, pulled in her chin and stood very straight, all the time glaring at Spunky. "And what was that horrible squawking I heard?"

Spunky's mouth dropped open. "I was singing."

"For a little girl, you have a very piercing voice."

Spunky felt like some kind of bug that was going to get stepped on. She took a deep breath and stood as tall as she could, lifting her head and staring right back. Let the old meanie gawk at my T-shirt she thought. It was one of her favorites, with I Love to Dance across the front.

If she practiced her dance steps and exercised she'd get stronger and when she got older, she'd audition for a dance show.

"Young lady." Mrs. Snodgrass looked down her nose. "The landlord informed me that a new tenant was moving in, but he didn't tell me the woman had a noisy child. What is your name?"

"It's Spunky," she said, hoping the old lady would ask about her nickname. She'd been a premature baby and the doctor didn't think she'd live, but she'd showed lots of spirit and spunk. So her parents nicknamed her Spunky. The name had stuck and she was proud of it.

The old lady shook her head. "No. What I want to know is your proper name."

"Oh, it's Sarah, Sarah Yvonne Crawford. But all my friends call me Spunky."

"Well, young lady, I will call you by your correct name. My surname is Snodgrass and you may address me as Mrs. Snodgrass."

"Okay." Spunky nodded, thinking Mrs. Snoop would be a much better name.

"Does your mother realize how foolish the name Spunky is going to sound when you grow up? Sarah Yvonne is much more ladylike. In fact, it's quite a lovely name."

So what? Right now she liked her nickname just fine.

"And you, young man." Mrs. Snodgrass turned to Sammy who'd been sitting quietly with his elbows resting on his knees.

"Uh, yes." Sammy's eyes widened as he peered through his straight black bangs. He got up slowly and extended his hand. "I'm Sammy Wong. How do you do?"

Spunky hoped Mrs. Snodgrass would notice that Sammy wasn't tall either. Height didn't matter unless you wanted to be a basketball player.

"Oh, well, yes, I'm pleased to meet you." Mrs. Snodgrass seemed surprised with Sammy's manners. She quickly shook his hand.

"Now young man, it's almost supper time and I'm sure your parents will be expecting you home."

Sammy backed up the stairs, one step at a time. Before he disappeared from Spunky's view, he shot her a quick glance. "See you at school tomorrow."

Spunky nodded. "Yeah."

Mrs. Snodgrass pushed back the cuff on her dress and checked her gold watch. "It's five o'clock. When your mother gets home the three of us need to review the rules for living in this house."

Spunky bowed her head and stared at her brand new shoes. Tapping had got her into trouble already.

Chapter Two

After she'd finished helping her mother clean the kitchen and do the supper dishes, Spunky stood on the landing and peered down the stairs. Nothing moved in the darkness below. Maybe the old ogre was out and she wouldn't have to apologize after all.

"Switch on the light," instructed her mother.

Brightness flooded the stairwell and basement. Spunky blinked and whispered. "I don't think she's home."

"Let's go." Her mother moved past her on the landing and started down the stairs.

Spunky followed. "Ten, nine, eight..." She was almost at the bottom.

"Three, two..." Just before Spunky could count any more the door of Mrs. Snodgrass' suite swung open and out stepped the old lady. She grimaced and clutched her purse closely to her chest.

"Hello, Mrs. Snodgrass," Mrs. Crawford said in a pleasant voice and Spunky felt pleased with her mom's cool attitude. "My daughter and I were just coming down to talk to you."

Spunky paused on the last step, wondering what the old lady would say.

"Can't talk to anyone now," snapped Mrs. Snodgrass. "I have to go out." She jerked the door shut and elbowed past Spunky's mom.

"This will just take a moment of your time," Mrs. Crawford placed her hand on the old lady's shoulder.

"Better make it fast. I have to get my groceries."

"Yes, I understand, but my daughter has something she wants to say."

Mrs. Snodgrass tightened her lips and her chin jutted out. "Hmmmph."

Standing on the bottom step, Spunky shifted her weight from one foot to the other and noticed that Mrs. Snodgrass was wearing the same dress as before. The old lady probably hadn't been sleeping this afternoon; she'd just wanted to complain about the noise.

Spunky took a deep breath and planted both feet firmly on the step. Standing as tall as she could, she lifted her head, but the words didn't come out.

"Spunky don't you have something you want to say?" Her mom raised her eyebrows.

"I...," Spunky started. The words caught in her throat. It wasn't fair that she was the one who had to apologize. She hadn't been doing anything wrong, both the upstairs and downstairs suites were supposed to share the washer and dryer. At least that's what she understood.

Mrs. Snodgrass stared at Spunky's jeans. The old lady's gaze stopped right at the knee where there was a big hole. Her lips tightened into a thin red line and she shook her head, muttering, "Children."

Mrs. Crawford cleared her throat and prompted Spunky, "My daughter has an apology."

Her mother's arms were folded across her chest and she started tapping one finger.

Spunky tried again, "I was dancing. I'm sorry," she said as fast as she could. Then she clamped her mouth shut and placed her hands on her hips. That was all she was going to say.

"I think what Spunky is trying to tell you is she's sorry she woke you earlier today."

"She has a very loud and piercing voice and tap shoes make a horrible racket." Mrs. Snodgrass puckered her lips like she'd tasted a sour lemon.

Spunky wanted to say. *And since I first met you this afternoon your voice has been high, squeaky and disapproving.*

"Well, my daughter does love to sing and she probably got a little carried away." Her mom gave her a warm smile and Spunky knew she understood.

"I can't have kids running around the basement. There are rules and she must learn them." Mrs. Snodgrass shook her finger. "She could bump into one of the furnaces and do damage."

Spunky cleared her throat, getting ready to ask how she could hurt either furnace when she hadn't been doing any running, but no one paid any attention.

"She won't do it again," replied Mrs. Crawford.

"The landlord wouldn't like it," continued Mrs. Snodgrass as if she hadn't heard a word. "I'll have to call Mr. Hansen and report it. He'll be very concerned over these events. He's very particular. Sarah won't want to get on the wrong side of him."

"Spunky will not be playing down here again."

"Mom," sputtered Spunky. "What do...?"

Spunky wasn't allowed to finish because her mother continued, "From now on Spunky will play upstairs, and she won't be singing or dancing."

"Good." Mrs. Snodgrass raised her chin, shoved past Spunky, and stomped up the stairs.

"Mommmmm," Spunky pleaded. Everything had gone wrong since she'd met Mrs. Snodgrass.

"That is enough, Sarah." Her voice sounded harsh, much harsher than Spunky had heard for a long time.

The outside door clicked shut. Spunky glanced up the stairs, wishing she'd never see the old lady again. Now she was out of the house Spunky hoped her mom would change her mind, but her serious look troubled Spunky. "Where can I dance?" she asked.

Mrs. Crawford didn't answer. She started up the steps. "We'll discuss it later."

Feeling defeated, Spunky trudged behind. In the kitchen she collapsed in a chair, rested her chin against her hands and waited.

Letting out a big sigh, Mrs. Crawford sat down and rested her arm on the table. "I can see we'll have to work very hard on getting along with Mrs. Snodgrass."

"What can I hurt in the basement?" Spunky frowned.

"Nothing," her mom replied. "However, Mrs. Snodgrass doesn't seem convinced. Right now we have to work on building goodwill with her."

"Huh." Spunky waved her arms. "How about if she builds some goodwill with us?"

Her mom put her hand over Spunky's. "At this time, I don't think that's going to happen so we'll have to be the ones to do it. Hopefully, if she sees that we are trying to be cooperative and friendly, she'll be less annoyed with you. I do not want the landlord receiving complaints about us."

Spunky felt badly for causing a problem but it really hadn't been her fault. In a low voice she said, "You know she's an old meanie who likes to complain."

"Sarah. You will not refer to her by any name other than Mrs. Snodgrass."

"Well, she is," muttered Spunky.

"And you will not be singing and dancing in the basement when Mrs. Snodgrass is home. We have to respect her privacy."

"But it's not *her* basement." Spunky pounded the table.

Her mom squeezed her hand and Spunky knew there was no use in arguing. She pulled her knee up to her chest and examined her sock. There was a tiny hole just starting and she pulled on the loose thread.

"Saraaaah."

Slowly she looked up. "Okay."

Then she looked down again. She couldn't just stop dancing, but she'd never lie to her mom. There had to be some way that she could dance and not cause her mother more trouble, but her mom hadn't said a word about playing in the basement when Mrs. Snodgrass was away.

Chapter Three

The next day after school, as soon as Mrs. Snodgrass left the house, Spunky went downstairs to practice her tap dancing. She laced her shoes.

Click.

Spunky froze. What was that noise?

A rattling sound echoed from the top of the stairs. Someone was up there, trying to open the outside door. Who was it? It couldn't be Mrs. Snodgrass. She'd just left.

"Ooooh noo, I'm in mega-trouble if she catches me down here," Spunky muttered. She looked around the basement. Where could she go? It was too late to run back upstairs. Before she could get through the door into the kitchen, she'd run smack into Mrs. Snodgrass on the landing.

Her heart slammed against her chest. *Hide*, she thought. *I've got to find some place to hide.* Any second now Snodgrass would have the inside door unlocked. If the old lady peered down the steps she'd spot Spunky. She scanned the basement. The washer and dryer were right against the wall. She couldn't squeeze behind them.

On the wall to the left of the machines was a cupboard, but it had a lock on it. Spunky rattled it, just in case. It held. She spun around. On the opposite side of the room, to the right of the door of Mrs. Snodgrass' suite, were two furnaces, one beside the other. Maybe, just maybe, she could squeeze into the small space behind the first one and once Mrs. Snodgrass was in her suite, she could easily escape.

The door handle squeaked. The hinges creaked and the door bumped against the stopper. Trying to keep her tap shoes quiet, Spunky dragged her feet. Five, giant, sliding steps and she was across the room. She took one last glance up the stairs, just before she squeezed between the furnace and the suite wall.

"Finally home." Mrs. Snodgrass' high-pitched voice echoed down the stairwell and into the basement.

Hardly daring to breathe, Spunky stood rigid.

Clunk, clunk, clunk. Mrs. Snodgrass thumped on each step. Sure she'd be discovered, Spunky sucked in her breath and edged to the left, and into the darkness. The furnace hummed and she brushed against the warm metal.

Mrs. Snodgrass reached the basement and searched in her purse.

If Spunky took a few steps and reached with her right arm she'd touch the old woman. Standing motionless, arms flat against her body, she held her breath. From her dark hiding place she watched Mrs. Snodgrass place the key in the lock.

Don't look at me, please don't look at me, she silently pleaded and turned her face away so any light wouldn't reflect off it and make her easier to see.

Finally the suite door banged shut.

Safe. Spunky sighed. *She never saw me.*

As quietly as possible she slid out from behind the furnace, removed her tap-shoes and tiptoed past Mrs. Snodgrass' door. She scampered up the ten steps to the landing, then three more steps and she was safe in the kitchen. Slumping into a chair, she rested her elbows on the table, her heart thumping.

Where was she going to dance?

Chapter Four

After Spunky and Sammy cycled through the park and down Jefferson Street they stopped in front of the bike shop.

Spunky stared at a bright, shiny pink bike in the window. "I'm going to get that." She pointed to the bike she had her heart set on.

"How?" asked Sammy.

"I don't know." Spunky stared at her friend. With his small round glasses and straight black hair, he reminded her of an owl, a very serious old owl. "Oh, lighten up."

Sammy sputtered, "I was just asking."

Spunky stamped her foot. "Wait and see. I'll do it somehow. I'll think of something." Glancing at her own bike, she noticed the chipped paint and crooked back fender. And even after all her scrubbing, the handlebars were still dirty.

Spunky pulled her bike closer to Sammy. "Look at this." She leaned over and wiggled the loose fender. "The last time I went over a bumpy road, I caught my foot on the chain-guard and now it's all crooked."

Sammy examined the chain and fender. "I see what you mean. But if your mom won't buy you a new bike, how do you think you'll get one? Besides, you said she couldn't afford it."

Her mom had enough to worry about with a new job and paying the rent. She didn't want to bother her about getting a new bike. "I'll just have to think up a plan."

"What?" Puzzled, Sammy tilted his head and eyed her.

"I don't know yet." Spunky paused. Right now she didn't have any ideas. "Something will happen. I'll get the money."

"Let's cycle to Loon Lake."

"Beat you," yelled Spunky as she placed her feet on the pedals, pushing as hard as she could, past parked cars on Jefferson and along streets that led to the top of the hill. The old bike squeaked and rattled.

When she reached the top, she was ahead of Sammy. Down below was Loon Lake and the campground on the other side. Dried leaves and gravel crunched as Sammy came up beside her.

"Took you long enough," Spunky teased.

"I needed to zip my jacket."

"Admit it Sammy. You're just slow. Beat you to the bottom." With the bike heading downhill, this was one race she could win without any head start.

The fender rattled over each tiny bump and Spunky gripped the handlebars to stay in control. Racing downhill the wind stung her face. She bit her lips and blinked to keep the swarms of tiny flies out of her mouth and eyes.

Once she got near the bottom, she pedaled hard. The next hill was long and steep. If she didn't have enough speed she'd slow down, and then Sammy with his ten-speed would come racing by her.

"Push, push," she prompted herself. Halfway up, she heard the tinkle of Sammy's bell and he shot past.

"See."

Spunky never heard the rest of what he said because the wind caught the words. But the flash of his red shirt whizzing by made her push harder. Little by little, she gained speed, and when she looked up she saw Sammy waiting for her.

As she neared him, he grinned, and said, "I'll give you a head start."

Spunky forced her legs to drive the pedals down. The wind nipped her face as she sailed along. Sammy zoomed by. She spied their stopping place. As she careened to the right, the bike frame shuddered and she pulled to a stop just off the path. She left her bike and walked down a narrow track to where Sammy was waiting for her at the edge of the lake.

Spunky picked up a flat rock and made it skip three times before it disappeared, with a splash, into the water.

Seeing Sammy choose a rock, she challenged him, "Hey, I'll bet I can make my rock skip more times than you can."

Sammy took aim. His rock skimmed along the surface and bounced four times before it sank.

Spunky eyed the rocks on the shore. She picked a smooth, flat one. With a side-arm she let it go.

"One, two, three," counted Sammy.

The rock continued to skip towards the far shore and Spunky joined in the counting, "Four, five." With a plunk, it too disappeared. "Beat that," bragged Spunky.

Sammy's next rock splashed closer to the shore and water splattered her face.

"You did that on..." Spunky shot a look at Sammy, but as she turned to accuse him, more water plinked on her face, and she realized it was starting to rain. The sky blackened.

"Let's get out of here," yelled Sammy, as he raced for his bike.

Spunky pedaled with all her might, the wind lashing her arms and face. Sammy raced ahead of her. Eager to get closer to Sammy, she forced her legs up and down, gaining speed.

Rocks crunched under the wheels. Spunky gripped the handlebars, struggling for control. She braked, but the bike didn't stop. Putting her feet down, she attempted to slow down. The bike lurched on its side and Spunky landed on her bare knees in the gravel.

Her leg throbbed. She pushed the bike away and used the back of her hand to wipe the blood away.

"You're hurt." Sammy pointed to her knees and then helped her to her feet.

"I'm okay." She brushed the rocks from her skin and up-righted her bike. Tears tickled the back of her throat. Drops of rain splashed her face.

A broken bike. Scratched legs. Could things get any worse?

Chapter Five

Once she and Sammy were inside the house, Spunky unlocked the door to the upper suite. "I'll get some towels." She hobbled through the kitchen and down the hall to where her mother kept the linens. She grabbed a towel and flung it at Sammy.

"Catch."

Sammy's hand shot out, retrieving the towel before it dropped to the ground.

Spunky grabbed another towel and rubbed her wet hair, trying to ignore her stinging legs.

"You'd better get a band aid on that knee," said Sammy.

"I will and I'll get you a hair dryer for your clothes," said Spunky, hoping Sammy would stay and keep her company.

"I'll only be a minute." She rushed into the bedroom, closed the door, changed her clothes and got a band aid from the bathroom.

Back in the kitchen, she asked Sammy, "What do you want to play?"

He gave the usual answer. "Monopoly."

Spunky frowned. "No. Let's play hide-and-go-seek. It's more fun."

"Where?" questioned Sammy. "It's raining outside."

She stalled. "Give me a minute."

Sammy continued in his sensible way. "We can't go in the basement, so just where can we play?"

"I'll think of something." Spunky scrunched up her face and pretended that she'd just come up with a new idea. "I've got it."

Sammy raised his eyebrows.

"The garage! It'll be great. I don't know why I didn't think of it before."

Snatching the towel from Sammy, she dumped the two damp ones in the laundry basket.

"What are we waiting for?" She took the garage key from the hook and tucked it in her jeans' pocket.

Outside, it was still pouring as she and Sammy sprinted down the sidewalk to the garage at the back of the property.

"Darn," she exclaimed, as she tried to twist the key in the old lock. "I can't get it open."

"Keep trying."

Rain splattered her face. After several attempts the lock popped open. Pushing the door back, she stepped inside, followed by Sammy. A ray of light flooded part of the dimly lit garage and particles of dust danced in the air.

Spunky sniffed. "Sure smells stale and dusty." She looked around. A wall separated the sides of the two-car garage so she couldn't see where her mom parked their car. Boxes, old windows and cases were stacked everywhere and on the end wall more junk leaned against the overhead door.

"Let's get some light in here." Sammy flicked the switch. Dim light warmed the place. "Wonder what's over there?" Sammy headed towards the opening.

"It's just my mom's car." Sammy disappeared and Spunky spotted a pile of interesting-looking boxes.

"There're lots of things over here," came Sammy's muffled voice from the far side.

"Yeah," agreed Spunky. Right now she wasn't very interested in what Sammy was saying. She'd made an interesting discovery.

Along the side wall were two old windows with thick wooden casings. Watching her reflection in the glass, she noticed that as she moved to the right, she could see the door. If she and Sammy played hide-and-go-seek, she could hide in a location where she'd be able to see the door in the window pane and Sammy would never guess her hiding place.

Sammy wandered back from the other side. "Let's play."

"What about hide-and-go-seek?" she asked, trying not to look smug. "Let's make the door home free." She kept a straight face.

"Sounds good to me," Sammy agreed.

"You're 'it.'"

Sammy turned his face to the wall and started counting. "Ten, nine..."

Now she could try out her plan. "Eight, seven six," called Sammy as Spunky tiptoed to the far end of the garage.

"Five, four..." His voice echoed off the walls.

Spunky ducked and slipped behind the large packing boxes.

"Three, two..."

Spunky crouched, and in the reflection from the glass she watched Sammy's back.

"One," announced Sammy. He spun around. "Coming. Ready or not."

At first he stayed close to 'Home Free' and appeared to be waiting for her. What did he think that she was going to do, jump out at him?

Carefully, Sammy edged away from the door and took a quick look behind some boxes. Next he moved towards her. Spunky held her breath.

"Where is she?" Spunky heard him whisper, and then he turned and disappeared into the other side.

This was her chance. She crawled out of her hiding place and darted across the garage. Positive that she was safe she bellowed, "Home."

Sammy appeared looking puzzled. "Where were you hiding?"

Spunky grinned. "That's my secret."

"I'll get you next time."

"Well, right now you're still 'it' so close your eyes and start counting."

"Ten, nine," Sammy's voice echoed.

Spunky stole to the end of the garage and crawled into her special hiding place. Settling against the cold cement floor she waited.

"Six, five, four," Sammy droned on.

Dust tickled her face. She pressed her finger against the tip of her nose and stopped a sneeze just in time.

Sammy had stopped counting.

The crunching of dead leaves on the floor told her Sammy was getting really close. She shrank into the darkness.

"Where is she?" muttered Sammy. His hand scraped against the boxes.

Spunky froze.

"Not here," he said.

The soft thump of his runners announced that he was leaving and she breathed a sigh of relief, relaxing on the cement. Above her, cobwebs hung and Spunky pulled on a silken thread. The outer part of the web broke away and she noticed that the rest of the web bounced back like a spring. The fine thread disappeared as she brushed her fingers against her jeans.

"Ah, ah...." She pushed on the tip of her nose, catching the sneeze just in time.

A quick glance at the window reflection told her that Sammy was still in the other part of the garage.

"Ah!" Spunky flinched. A huge daddy long legs spider crawled up her leg. Spunky flicked it with her fingers and at the same moment she sneezed. AHHCHOOO. The sound bounced off the walls and ceiling, echoing through the garage.

In a flash Spunky crawled out of her hiding place.

"Got you!" yelled Sammy.

Spunky slammed into the door at the same time as Sammy.

Sammy turned to Spunky. "Gesundheit."

"You'd never have caught me if I hadn't sneezed."

"But you did."

"We tied getting here," Sammy protested. "Tie goes to the person who's 'it.'"

"Okay," Spunky reluctantly agreed. She leaned against the wall. "You can have your turn then let's do something more exciting."

"You only want to stop playing because you lost." Sammy gave her his wise-owl expression.

Spunky pointed at all the boxes and her eyes gleamed. "Wouldn't you just love to know what's inside?"

"Sure," shrugged Sammy. "But they're not ours."

"Instead of playing another game, why don't we look?"

"Okay, you stay here and check out these boxes. There's something I'd like to examine." Sammy disappeared into the other side of the garage while Spunky busied herself with lifting the lid on a box. Before she had time to check the contents, she heard scraping and creaking, followed by a thump.

Spunky froze. "Are you okay, Sammy?"

"Wow."

The excitement in his voice caught Spunky's attention and she jumped up. As she rounded the corner, she saw Sammy holding onto a rope. In front of him was a ladder that seemed to have dropped from the ceiling.

"Look at this." He pointed to a big square hole above him.

"Cool, I wonder what's up there?" said Spunky.

"I've never seen anything like this." Sammy's eyes were big and round.

"What are we waiting for?" Spunky placed her foot on the first rung and started to climb.

After eight steps she poked her head through the opening and saw a big attic with more piles of boxes. "Sammy, wait till you see this."

"Maybe I could if you'd keep moving," said Sammy from below.

"I am." Quickly, Spunky stepped onto the attic floor

A few seconds later Sammy stood beside her, his mouth open.

"Did you turn on the light?" A single bare light bulb hung from the ceiling, casting eerie shadows behind the boxes stacked in the center of the attic.

"I flicked the switch just inside the garage door. I would assume that all the lights are connected on one circuit," Sammy replied, showing his usual logic.

"Of course." She patted Sammy on the back. For a minute it'd flashed through her head that *something* had turned on the light.

On all sides of the attic, boxes were stacked against the walls and some piles almost reached the sloped roof. Because she and Sammy were short, they could stand upright in the center section.

"Who do you think owns all this?" Sammy whispered.

"Probably Mr. Hansen, the landlord."

"Wow, he sure has a lot of stuff. I wonder why it's here."

"I bet he doesn't want it and nobody cares about it." Spunky swiped her finger over the top of a box and held it out so Sammy could see the dust. "Let's open a few?"

"But they're not ours. You shouldn't snoop through boxes that don't belong to you."

"Oh Sammy. It's not that big a deal. All we'll do is look."

Sammy wrinkled his nose.

Spunky knew she'd have to convince him. "We'll put everything back and besides, we won't hurt anything."

Seeing the unsure expression, she continued, "Who'd want this stuff anyways? They left it in a garage."

"Well...maybe," Sammy reluctantly agreed.

"It's probably all old junk, so who'd care?"

Sammy shrugged. "I guess nobody."

Spunky grinned. "What are we waiting for?"

Chapter Six

"Where do we start?" asked Sammy.

A shiver of excitement ran down Spunky's spine as she glanced around. Boxes, books and chairs were stacked against the walls that sloped and touched the floor. In one corner Spunky spotted a battered brown trunk.

"Look at this." She walked over and kneeled down. The leather straps were old and brittle.

Running her hand over the top of the trunk, Spunky felt the rough wood. "I wonder how old it is. Can you imagine all the adventures it's had?"

She stretched her hand out so Sammy could see the dirt. "Here's more proof that nobody's interested in all this stuff. We're the first people who've been here in goodness knows how long."

"Most likely been sitting here all its life," Sammy responded in his usual matter-of-fact tone.

"No. I bet it was on a pirate ship."

Sammy rolled his eyes, "Yeah, sure. Tell me how it got all the way to Badger Creek, Montana?"

Hoping to deter his logic, Spunky pointed. "Look at the floor."

Sammy shrugged and glanced down. "So what am I supposed to see?"

"Nothing. That's just it. No one's been here. There are no footprints in the dust."

"Probably because nobody wants the stuff and they dumped it up here."

"I know there's something valuable inside."

Sammy crossed his arms over his chest. "How do you know that?"

Spunky put her hand over her heart. "I have a feeling. In here."

She made a wide sweep with her hand. "This whole attic is going to become our treasure. Maybe when I open the lid we'll find piles of gold. Spanish doubloons. It might be a lost treasure and we'll be rich. I'll buy the bike and you can do whatever you want with your half of the money."

"Yeah, sure, and all these boxes have more gold in them," Sammy replied, skeptically.

"Well, how do you know? People are still finding treasures that were lost a long time ago."

"That's only in the movies."

"Really, Sammy, I read about some people who found a whole treasure ship of gold in the Caribbean. They'd been searching for years and years and nobody believed there was any treasure, but they found chests of gold."

"That was in a ship sunk in the ocean, not in an attic."

"Let's start here." As she knelt in front of the trunk Spunky hoped there'd be something of value. "Don't you ever dream that you'll find something worth lots of money? Think about it. If there's a fortune in rubies and diamonds, my mom could buy a house and we'd move far away from crabby old Snodgrass."

"My mom always tells me not to hold my breath."

Spunky frowned. "What do you mean?"

"She means that it's probably not going to happen, so I might as well not wait for it."

"Hah." Spunky scoffed. "Adults aren't right all the time, and she hasn't seen our attic. I know it's special."

"Come on." Spunky motioned for Sammy to squat. "Let's open this together." The rusty hinges groaned and squeaked. She closed her eyes and waited. Then, when the creaking stopped, she whispered, "What's in it?"

"Look for yourself."

Spunky opened her eyes and peered into the trunk. Disappointment trickled through her. "Oh, no, just old clothes." She touched the top layer. The white material was silky and smooth. She carefully lifted it out. "Here, hold this while I search the bottom. Maybe something's hidden underneath."

Stretching over the edge, Spunky pushed her hand down the inside. She felt around but there was nothing but more clothes. She sighed and withdrew her hand. "We can take another look at these later." Having lost interest in the trunk, she piled the clothing back inside. "Let's check the boxes."

Spunky kneeled beside a stack marked, books, china, dishes, and encyclopedias.

Sammy wandered away while Spunky opened a heavy unlabeled box. To her disappointment all she found was a stack of Popular Mechanics. A lump formed in her throat as she lifted one magazine then another. They were all about fifty years old with pictures of old cars on the covers. Her dad had collected copies of this magazine and he'd probably consider these collectors' items. The pain deepened in her chest. Her dad would never have a chance to enjoy what she'd found.

"I think I've got something." Sammy's muffled voice snapped Spunky out of her thoughts.

Spunky glanced around the attic. "Where are you?"

Crouched over, Sammy appeared from behind a pile of boxes. "Look what I found," he said, grinning.

Cradled in his arms was a blue box and Spunky figured it was about ten inches deep.

"It sure is heavy." Sammy carefully placed it on the floor.

"Let's open it." Spunky sat and pulled the box towards her. "Look at this. Someone wrapped ribbon around it and they even tied a bow at the top."

She untied the knot and pulled off the lid. Tissue paper was tightly stuffed around something. After unwrapping the paper, she took out two creamy-colored horsehead bookends.

Sammy reached over and touched them. "Wow, they're nice. I wonder what's in the other boxes."

"What are we waiting for? Let's get them." In a flash Spunky was up on her feet and in the corner of the attic searching for more fancy blue containers. One by one she handed them to Sammy. "Here, put them in the center where it's not so dusty, and then we can open everything."

Half an hour later, sitting in the middle of her discoveries, Spunky surveyed the dishes, books, ornaments, and other items scattered on the floor.

"See, we've found treasure."

Sammy raised his eyebrows. "We have?"

"Sure, it's all here." Spunky spun around and clutched Sammy's shoulder. "Look." She pointed to the boxes. "This is the treasure."

"I don't see any gold or jewels."

"That's what I thought at first. But it doesn't have to be gold. We can make money from all this." Spunky waved her arms, indicating the boxes. "We can sell everything."

"You can't sell it," corrected Sammy.

"Why not?"

"Because it's not yours."

"Then whose is it?" said Spunky.

"I don't know."

"Well, we rent the garage and it's in here," argued Spunky, trying to convince herself.

"I know, but maybe it belongs to the owner. You said that yourself." Sammy still seemed unsure.

"You mean old Mr. Hansen, the landlord? But, but..." protested Spunky. "You can tell all this stuff has been here for ages, so he wouldn't want it."

"All I'm saying is that you'd better check and find out who owns it," explained Sammy.

Spunky had a sinking feeling in her stomach. You just couldn't sell things that belonged to somebody else. That would be stealing. No matter how hard she tried to convince herself, she knew Sammy was right. She paced back and forth over the creaking, wooden floor.

Suddenly she stopped. "Sammy, I've got an idea."

Sammy scrunched his face.

"I think we can do it."

"How?" He raised his eyebrows reminding her, once again, of a wise old owl.

"Oh, why didn't I think of this before? I'll get my mom to phone Mr. Hansen and if he doesn't care about all this stuff, then we can sell it at a garage sale."

"What garage sale?" Sammy eyebrows shot up and his eyes widened.

"The one we're going to have. We'll sell everything and I'll make enough money to buy my new bike." Spunky held her breath, waiting for Sammy's approval.

Sammy nodded. "Sure. Why not?"

"Good." Spunky jumped up and started down the ladder. "My mom will be home soon. Let's ask her."

Sammy looked at his watch. "Can't," he said. "I have to go home for supper."

"Okay, see ya tomorrow," called Spunky as she locked the garage. She raced to the house, hoping her mom was back already so she could make the phone call to Mr. Hansen and get his okay.

Chapter Seven

A few minutes later Mrs. Crawford arrived home and Spunky hit her with the question. "Mom," she asked breathlessly. "I found some great stuff. Can I sell it?"

Her mother hung her coat in the closet. "And hello to you, too," she said. She didn't answer Spunky's question, but just put her arms around Spunky and gave her a kiss on the forehead. "How's my girl?"

"Fine, fine," replied Spunky, wiggling out of her mother's arms. "Things are great."

There was a puzzled look on her mother's face. "Honey, I'm delighted that things are great, but would you mind explaining to me what made you change your mind so quickly?"

"Can I sell everything?"

"Spunky, what does everything being great and you selling things have to do with each other? Are you planning on selling all your toys?"

"No." Spunky was shocked. "You didn't think I'd do that?"

Her mom smiled. "I'm just teasing. I know how much you love your books and games."

"Oh." Spunky heaved a sigh of relief. "You had me scared."

"Now, what is it you want to sell?"

"We found some great things in the attic in the garage. You should see the stuff: china, ornaments, and all sorts of things."

"And you want to sell them?"

"Yeah, then I can use the money for a bike. It's a great idea."

"One problem, Spunky, those things don't belong to us, so how can you sell them?"

"Well, that's it, I figured they must belong to Mr. Hansen, and he probably wouldn't care if we sold everything."

"Well…" Her mom hesitated. "I don't know if that's such a good idea."

"Couldn't you phone him and ask?"

Her mom looked doubtful, so Spunky added, "You could tell him I'd clean out the garage, then I'd have a place to dance."

"All right, you've convinced me," her mom relented. "I'll give him a phone call."

"Phone him right now."

Mrs. Crawford put up her hand. "Have some patience. I just got home from work and I'm a little late. I'd like to get supper started. Besides, Mr. Hansen is probably eating and doesn't want to be disturbed."

"Ah, gee," moaned Spunky.

The rest of the night Spunky waited for her mom to phone the landlord and before she went to bed she reminded her mom again. "You haven't forgotten, have you?"

"No, Spunky." Her mother stopped writing and looked up from the small desk in the nook. "I just want to get all these checks written so I can mail them tomorrow."

Spunky looked at the clock on the cupboard above the sink. "But it's getting late."

Her mother glanced at the clock.

"He might be in bed," added Spunky.

"Spunky, I really don't think that Mr. Hansen would be in bed by nine o'clock."

"You won't forget?"

"No, I won't, and that reminds me it's time for you to take your bath."

"I had one yesterday," Spunky protested.

"I know young lady, but you were playing in the garage and it hasn't been cleaned. Right?"

"Yeah."

Spunky dragged her feet all the way to the bathroom. She crossed her fingers. If only Mr. Hansen would say yes, then she'd get enough money to buy the bike.

Chapter Eight

Spunky stretched in bed and listened to the birds chirping outside her window. Today she and Sammy were going to search through the boxes in the attic. She jumped out of bed, grabbed her clothes and dressed. Then she raced down the hall.

"What's the hurry?" asked her mom as Spunky screeched to a halt in the kitchen.

"What did Mr. Hansen say? Can I sell the stuff? Is it his? I want to start on it after school today."

Mrs. Crawford put down the orange she was peeling and held up her hand. "Hold it, I only have two ears. I wasn't able to get hold of Mr. Hansen last night."

"Oh no. Maybe he went to bed early and that's why he didn't answer the phone."

"Judging by the number of times I let the phone ring, I think he would have answered."

"Then why didn't you keep calling?"

"I did, five or six times, but he must have been out."

"Doesn't he have voicemail? Almost everybody has it."

"Apparently he doesn't. I'll call him from work."

"Good." Spunky hoped she'd get an answer.

"And in the meantime, I would ask that until we get his permission you don't touch anything else."

"Ah, gee mom," complained Spunky. "Can't I just sort them?"

"No. Give me time to talk to him and then we'll get an answer for sure. I think you can wait until I get home tonight."

"But that's such a long wait."

***

After class, Spunky walked out of the school yard with Sammy. "Can you come to my house?"

"Can't," replied Sammy, hitching his backpack higher on his shoulders.

"I'll play Monopoly," she added, hoping to change Sammy's mind because the board game was one of his favorites.

"My mom said I have to get home, right away."

"Okay," Spunky sighed, feeling downhearted. She'd be all alone. There were times when she wished her mom got home earlier.

At home, Spunky sat at the kitchen table doing her homework and wondering if her mom had talked to Mr. Hansen. Since she couldn't go and sort the treasures in the garage, she'd just have to wait.

She wondered if she should phone and ask, but she remembered that she was only supposed to call her mom at work if there was a major problem. Finding out if mom got hold of Mr. Hansen wasn't exactly an emergency.

Tap, tap-pe-ty-tap. Spunky beat a syncopated rhythm with her feet. She stared at the clock. "Hurry up, mom," she mumbled and glanced at the closed door to the landing. What was Mrs. Snodgrass doing?

Cautiously opening the door, Spunky listened for sounds from the basement. Nothing. Mrs. Snodgrass must be out. Silently, she stepped down the three steps to the landing beside the back door. Bending her knees, she peered down the stairs, once again reassuring herself that nobody was there. Why not practice a few tap steps? If Mrs. Snodgrass did come home she'd hide until the old meanie went into her suite. Then, when the path was clear, she'd sneak back upstairs.

A minute later, Spunky tiptoed down the stairs clutching her precious black taps. She passed Mrs. Snodgrass' door and sat on the floor, ready to lace her shoes.

Thump. Spunky froze. The sound came from Mrs. Snodgrass' suite. With a feeling of horror, Spunky watched as the door handle started to twist and the door swung partially open. Then it stopped, and she heard Mrs. Snodgrass.

"Darn. I forgot the soap."

Without a second to spare Spunky jumped up, grabbed her shoes and squeezed behind the furnace. From her hiding space she heard a clunk and she shrank into the shadows.

"I'll get my laundry done before the little terror from upstairs gets home."

"The little terror." Spunky muttered. "How dare she call me that?"

Spunky edged a fraction to her right and cautiously peered around the corner.

Busy picking her dirty laundry out of the basket, Mrs. Snodgrass was bent over, with her back to Spunky. She dropped some clothes into the washing machine and left others in a pile on the floor.

"Oh!" exclaimed Mrs. Snodgrass. "Where's my apron? I must have left it on the table."

Now's my chance to get out of here, thought Spunky. But no sooner was Mrs. Snodgrass into her suite and then she was out with another pile of laundry.

The water gurgled and sprayed into the washing machine. Spunky waited for Mrs. Snodgrass to leave.

"This place is so untidy." The old lady's squeaky voice bounced off the heating pipes.

What's she doing now? Spunky didn't dare peek. Mrs. Snodgrass might spot her.

"The mess some people leave."

Spunky wondered if Mrs. Snodgrass was looking at the two boxes that she'd shoved under the steps.

"Really, what kind of a mother would allow her daughter to keep such junk?"

Junk! Spunky's face felt hot.

"What's this? That woman is too lax with that child."

Don't you say that about my mom, Spunky wanted to yell. She's the best mom in the whole world.

"Really," commented Mrs. Snodgrass as if she'd heard Spunky.

Yes, the B-E-S-T.

"Now, what have we here?"

There was silence, and Spunky strained to hear what was happening.

"Well..."

There was a long pause.

"Who is this?"

You leave my stuff alone, Spunky longed to scream.

"He's handsome."

Spunky knew it. Mrs. Snodgrass had opened her box and was snooping through the pictures. Touching them and making fingerprints. How dare the old busybody nose through her favorite pictures of her dad?

"No wonder you left. I'd leave too if I had such a little terror."

He didn't leave me. The thoughts choked in Spunky's throat. *My dad would never have left us.*

"Spunky. What an unsuitable name for a girl."

Spunky wanted to blast out of her hiding place and yell, *leave my pictures alone. Get your boney old hands off them. My dad never left us.* But she clenched her fists, gritted her teeth and waited.

"My, my, I wonder where he went." Mrs. Snodgrass' voice jarred Spunky.

She remembered her mother crying and holding her very tight. Spunky choked and blinked, fighting to hold back the tears. On a cold, rainy night two years ago her dad was on his way home, but he never made it. Another driver who'd been drinking was speeding through a red light and smashed right into her dad's car, on the driver's side. "That's why he isn't here and we have to live in this house with horrible you," she murmured.

The washing machine grumbled and thumped to a stop.

"I'd better get the clothes in the dryer," muttered Mrs. Snodgrass.

Spunky shifted her weight from one foot to the other. How long was it going to be before she could escape? It felt like she'd been hiding forever.

Chapter Nine

Spunky squirmed in her narrow hiding space. Wasn't Mrs. Snodgrass ever going to leave? Why didn't she go back to her suite? She didn't need to stand and watch her clothes.

Spunky's legs and arms were hot. She longed to sit down, but most of all she just wanted to get upstairs.

"Look at these scuff marks," complained Mrs. Snodgrass. "I'll get rid of them."

The swish-swash of the mop told Spunky that Mrs. Snodgrass had started scrubbing the floor.

Booooom! Spunky jumped. The side of the furnace vibrated. Mrs. Snodgrass must have bumped it with the mop. Now the swish-swash was closer and the smell of the cleaning solution tickled her nose. What if Mrs. Snodgrass tried to wash where she was hiding? The old lady would find her for sure.

In desperation, Spunky squeezed left, past the second furnace and into a larger space that looked like a closet. Straight ahead was a door. Dull light filtered through the slats and the crack at the bottom. On her left and right were unfinished walls. She could see the upright wooden boards that were usually covered by drywall and paint. Probably nobody used this closet and only someone small could get into the narrow space. But where did the door lead?

Cautiously, she placed her hand on the knob and slowly twisted. Easing the door open a crack she could see across a hallway and into a bedroom. Her heart pounded as she silently stepped into the hall. She tiptoed into the bedroom. Stuffed animals and toys were lined up on the bed. Sitting on a nearby chair was a grey squirrel with sparkling eyes. In his paws was a real peanut. Spunky stroked the soft fur.

Hardly believing what she saw, Spunky shook her head. "You can't belong to mean old Snodgrass. Why would she have anything as cute as you?"

Silently the animals stared back at her.

She picked up a pale pink bear with a yellow stomach and brushed the bear's silky-smooth fur against her face.

"Where did she find you? You're too cuddly to live with her."

"All done."

Hearing a voice from outside the suite, Spunky placed the bear on the bed, scampered out of the room and back into the closet.

Just as she shut the door Mrs. Snodgrass said, "Who's there?"

Holding her breath, Spunky stood very still.

"Is anybody there?" The voice was louder.

If Snodgrass opened the closet door and saw her, she'd be grounded for months.

She had to escape.

Chapter Ten

Spunky gazed around the garage attic. She could hardly believe her good fortune as she looked at the piles of china, books and ornaments that were scattered on the floor.

"I'm so excited," she exclaimed. "Just think, Sammy, we can sell all of this neat stuff."

Sammy didn't reply. Spunky frowned. "Where are you, Sammy? Are you hiding?"

A muffled reply came from the corner. "I'm over here."

Peering around a pile of boxes, Spunky saw Sammy squatting on the floor. "What're you doing down there?"

Sammy wiggled out, stood up and proudly showed a box he'd found. "This was hidden. I didn't see it before."

"Let's open it."

He handed her the blue box.

"It's heavy." Spunky sat down on the floor. Carefully she untied the gold ribbon and lifted the lid.

"They sure put lots of tissue in here." Piece by piece, she removed the tissue until a gleaming red and white-striped tent top appeared.

"What is it?" Sammy leaned over Spunky.

Now Spunky had removed all the pieces of tissue, and she gently lifted a tiny merry-go-round from the box.

"It's beautiful."

"Let me look at it." Sammy put out his hands.

"Careful," warned Spunky. "It's very fragile. Look at these little horses." Spunky ran her fingers over the smooth, shiny surface of one of the horses. There were six in all: two black, two greys and two white. Each horse was attached to a silver pole that came from underneath the canopy. The saddles were decorated with swirls and flowers.

"I think it winds up. If I turn this knob it will..."

"No, no." Spunky pushed Sammy's hand away. "I'll do it."

Slowly, she twisted the knob half a turn to the right and placed the carousel on the floor. The little horses started to move around in a circle. From the bottom of the ornament came a pleasant tinkling melody.

"A musical carousel," exclaimed Sammy. "You'll get lots of money for this."

"No." Spunky watched the horses stop moving and a second later the music stopped. "I won't sell it. I'm going to put it in my bedroom. At night I'll listen to the music."

Sammy wrinkled his nose. "Are you sure Mr. Hansen said you could sell everything?"

"I'm sure." She knew exactly where the carousel would sit on her night table.

"He insisted we'd be doing him a favor by cleaning out this old attic." Spunky repeated what her mother had told her. "We got permission and I'm going to sell it all." Then she gazed at the carousel. "But not this."

Sammy shook his head. "I still don't get it. Who'd leave this in a garage? It must belong to somebody."

"Nobody wants it or they wouldn't have left it here. So it's mine now," said Spunky, trying to convince herself.

"Sammy, why don't you take something that you like?"

"I don't know," Sammy paused. "I don't feel right about it."

"Oh, don't be a spoilsport. We're going to sell everything we can so why shouldn't you have something?"

"I'll wait and see."

There was no changing Sammy's mind once it was made up, so she didn't try. She twisted the knob on the bottom of the carousel again and the tiny horses moved up and down while the melody tinkled.

But no matter how hard she tried she couldn't forget Sammy's question. Whose carousel had it been? And more important, why had it been hidden in the attic?

Chapter Eleven

The next day Spunky and Sammy were back in the garage attic.

Sammy waved his arm indicating the stacks of books, china and ornaments. "Are you sure Mr. Hansen said we could sell all this?"

Spunky couldn't help but grin as she surveyed their treasures. They'd have the sale, make lots of money and she'd buy a new bike. Sammy could do whatever he wanted with his half of the money. "Well, my mom phoned Mr. Hansen and he said he'd be really happy if someone got some use out of this stuff, especially if we clean everything."

Sammy shrugged. "It's strange."

"You know what's strange, Sammy?"

He shook his head. "No."

"Mrs. Snodgrass. She's really weird. She's a neat freak and she even talks to herself. She's got tons of stuffed animals, all lined up on her bed and piles of them in a chair. I mean why would an old meanie like her have all that stuff?"

"Beats me," Sammy shrugged and eyed her doubtfully. "How do you know so much about Mrs. Snodgrass?"

"Why should I tell?" She enjoyed keeping Sammy guessing.

"Were you spying on her?"

"Maybe." She'd let him guess, until he got the right answer.

"You were listening outside her door. Weren't you?" Sammy grinned, pleased that he thought he'd figured it out. "What if she opened her door and caught you?"

Spunky chuckled. "That can't happen."

"You sound pretty sure of yourself. If you are spying on her and you get caught, you'll really be in big trouble."

"Won't happen."

"Why not?"

"Because she can't see me." Spunky tapped her feet as she danced around some boxes. She stopped. "So what do you think?"

"Sounds interesting."

"Do you want to see the secret hiding place I've found?"

Chapter Twelve

Disappointed that Sammy had to go home, Spunky stood at the kitchen counter, talking to her mom on the phone.

"I'm okay. You don't have to rush home," Spunky reassured her mom. "I've still got some homework to do. Bye, bye." Spunky placed the telephone back on its cradle and slumped onto a chair.

She stared at her math assignment. The last thing she felt like doing was homework. Through the open window Spunky heard birds chirping. Their sound was abruptly interrupted by a noise from the outside door.

"Where is it?" Mrs. Snodgrass' impatient voice prompted Spunky to stand up and move silently to the window. She peeked through the space between the curtains. There, on the side door step, stood Mrs. Snodgrass with her head bent as she searched for something in her purse.

Probably she's looking for her key, thought Spunky.

"Don't tell me I've lost it." Mrs. Snodgrass sounded more annoyed. She shoved her hand back in her purse and Spunky imagined her bony fingers reaching into every corner.

Wondering if she should open the door, Spunky leaned closer to see if Mrs. Snodgrass had found her key. Bump. Her head knocked the window pane.

"What's that?" Mrs. Snodgrass' head snapped up. She scowled at Spunky. "Why are you staring at me?"

"Uh." Spunky drew back.

"Does your mother know you've been spying?"

Spunky gasped. Had Mrs. Snodgrass figured out that she'd watched her from the closet?

Mrs. Snodgrass flicked her hand, like Spunky was an annoying insect. "Go away and mind your own affairs."

Spunky peered back at the woman. "I was going to open the door for you."

"Don't bother." She pulled a set of keys out of her purse.

Spunky let the curtain drop. The back door banged. Mrs. Snodgrass thumped down the stairs and there was one last bang, indicating the lower suite door was closed.

Spunky turned on the kitchen tap and poured herself a glass of water. She gulped down the cold liquid and glanced at the clock. Five fifteen. Her mom wouldn't be home until six o'clock. If...if she was really quiet, maybe she could sneak down the stairs and see what Mrs. Snodgrass was doing. She hesitated for a minute. What if she got caught? No, she'd be super quiet. Snodgrass wouldn't hear anything.

She quickly pulled off her shoes and socks so she wouldn't make a sound. In her bare feet, she crept down the stairs, then squeezed behind the first furnace and inched her way past the second one. Finally she was in the closet with her nose lightly touching the door. She held her breath.

"Eight hundred, eight hundred and fifty, nine hundred." Mrs. Snodgrass sat on the sofa with her back to the closet door, counting out money onto the living room coffee table.

Spunky watched her pick up the bills and place them into a white envelope. The old lady glanced around the room, and then she went to the wall unit and pulled out a book. She placed the envelope between the pages and placed the book back on the shelf.

Why was the old lady hiding her money? What a weird thing to do.

"There, now I have as much as I need." Mrs. Snodgrass patted the spine of the book. "My money is safe."

That's crazy, thought Spunky. Why does she keep so much money down here? Doesn't she know there are banks?

"Time for supper." Mrs. Snodgrass walked within a foot of Spunky. She held her breath, hoping the old lady wouldn't open the door.

Pots and pans rattled in the kitchen.

Thinking it was safe to scamper upstairs, Spunky squeezed past the furnaces and was ready to step into the open when the suite door banged and Mrs. Snodgrass charged into the laundry room.

"I forgot the bedding. They'll be all wrinkled." Mrs. Snodgrass opened the dryer door and pulled out sheets.

Spunky gasped and moved further into the darkness. She waited. She heard the dryer door clanging shut. Her heart hammered against her chest. She'd better stay put until she was certain Mrs. Snodgrass had all her laundry. Who knew how long that would take? She could only hope that her mom wouldn't come home in the meantime.

She glanced around her hiding space. Propped against the wall was a tall, skinny box. Inside Spunky found two baseball bats.

Why does she have these? Spunky pulled one out and ran her fingers down the smooth wooden finish. I could really slug a home run with this, she thought. Fat chance. The old lady would never give her one. But why would she even hide bats in her closet.

Spunky started to place the bat back, but the box shifted and bumped the wall.

"What was that?" Mrs. Snodgrass' sharp voice made Spunky's blood freeze. She was headed for big trouble.

Through the slats of the door she saw a shadow. She shrank against the wall and watched with horror as the doorknob slowly started to twist.

The hinges on the door creaked. "Oh, no." This time she'd really done it. She was going to be caught for sure. What should she do?

The phone rang.

"Who's' trying to sell me something now?" Mrs. Snodgrass closed the door and Spunky sank against the wall and heaved a sigh of relief. Thank goodness for telephone soliciting. She wouldn't get caught.

Chapter Thirteen

The alarm buzzed and Spunky smacked the top of it. She leaped out of bed and pulled on a T-shirt and jeans.

"Spunky! Breakfast is ready," her mom called from the kitchen.

"Coming," yelled Spunky. She charged into the bathroom and splashed warm water over her face. Back in the bedroom she searched under the bed for her runners. Then with her laces flapping, she scurried down the hall.

At the kitchen table, she pulled out her chair, sat down and grabbed the orange sections from her plate.

"And good morning to you too."

Spunky gulped down the last piece of orange and looked over at her mother who was standing at the sink. "Hi, Mom."

"What are you so hyper about?"

"Today's the garage sale. I told Sammy to be here at eight-thirty."

Spunky stuffed the bottom half of the bran muffin into her mouth and licked her fingers. "We've got tons to do."

"I don't know if you should have the garage sale today." Her mom looked worried.

"We're all ready. Why shouldn't we have it?"

"Spunky, if you'll just listen for a few seconds, I'll explain." Her mom put down the towel, pulled out a chair and sat at the table. "The reason I was thinking that you should change it to next weekend is because I have to go into work today."

Spunky tapped her foot on the floor and glared at her mother. She was going to spoil all their plans. "Why are you going to work on Saturday?"

"Some documents came into the office yesterday and I have to get them ready for Monday."

"But why should I cancel the garage sale?"

"Because I won't be here if anything goes wrong."

"Mom, I'm not a baby." Spunky got up abruptly, collecting dirty dishes. Plates and cutlery clattered as she opened the dishwasher and shoved them inside. Finally she turned to her mother who looked sad. "Mom, it's not that I don't want you here. I didn't mean that. It's just that Sammy and I can take care of ourselves."

"Oh, Spunky." Her mother put her tea cup back on the saucer. "I've been so concerned about you. Since we moved to Badger Creek I've worked long hours. I don't like to leave you alone so much."

"It's okay." Spunky walked over to the table and wrapped her arms around her mother, snuggling into her and feeling warm and secure. "Sammy and I are fine." Spunky stepped back. "What could go wrong?"

"My little girl. You're growing up so fast, but I still worry about you. Things haven't worked out quite like I thought they would. I was hoping we'd be friends with Mrs. Snodgrass and that when I was at work she could keep an eye on you."

Having Mrs. Snodgrass babysit horrified Spunky. She gave her mom a big hug "I'm okay by myself. You worry too much."

"I'll try not to." Her mom laughed and put her hands out, palms up. "It's a simple garage sale, isn't it? Like you said, what can go wrong? But just to keep me happy, will you phone me in an hour and let me know how you are?"

"Sure," she replied, pleased that her mom trusted her.

"What time are you going to start?"

"One o'clock sharp."

"I'll try to be home as close to one as I can then." Her mom picked up her purse and opened the door. "Have a good morning dear." Her mom gave her a quick kiss on the forehead.

"Bye, Mom," yelled Spunky as the back door clicked shut.

After Spunky finished tidying the kitchen, she pocketed the house keys and went outside. Seeing Sammy walking down the street, she sprinted across the lawn and joined him at the garage. After unlocking the door, she and Sammy stepped inside. "Those must be the tables mom told me Mr. Hansen said he'd loan us for the sale."

"They're huge. When did they arrive?" asked Sammy.

"Must have been after I got to sleep last night."

"Let's get the tables out of here first." Spunky lifted one end and Sammy got the other. They edged it through the door and out onto the lawn.

When they'd finished lugging the other tables outside, Sammy wiped his hands across the back of his jeans. "Where's your mom?"

"She had to go to work." Seeing Sammy's worried expression Spunky added, "That's okay. I told her we could do it ourselves."

"It would have been nice if she could have been here."

"Oh, Sammy, you just worry too much. Now let's get everything out of the garage and start putting on the prices."

After dozens of trips, all the items were finally arranged on the four tables. For the next few hours she and Sammy attached price tags to everything and soon it was time for the sale to start.

Spunky reached in a box under the table to retrieve the gorilla costume she'd been saving for Sammy. She pulled it out and held it up for him to get the full effect. "This is for you."

"I'm not wearing that?"

Spunky waved her finger at him. "Listen, if you don't go to Main Street and get the people's attention how are we ever going to sell anything?"

Sammy wrinkled his nose. "I'm going to look pretty silly."

"Nobody will know it's you. Besides, you want me to get a better bike? Don't you?"

"Sure I do."

"Then you have to wear this." Spunky pulled a mask from another box. "Isn't it great?"

Sammy screwed up his face and shook his head. "No, I won't. I won't wear that gorilla mask. Why can't I just hold the garage sale sign?"

"Cause the outfit along with the mask will really get people's attention. Just imagine the interest you'll attract when people see a gorilla on the sidewalk."

"Well, why don't you wear it instead of me?"

"It'll be my turn later. Come on, Sammy, you've got to wear it. Please? I'll stand at the tables and sell for the first shift, then it will be your turn and I'll do it."

Sammy stepped into the costume. Spunky helped him pull the sign over his head and then she positioned the gorilla headpiece.

"Where's the flag?" asked Sammy in a muffled voice.

Spunky pulled out a tattered piece of red cloth on a stick.

Handing it to Sammy, she said, "Don't forget to wave this and point it so the cars know to turn right at the corner. Then they'll see our tables."

Sammy nodded. The mask wiggled up and down as he clomped towards the intersection. He crossed the street and Spunky watched him raise his arms and wave the red flag.

At first, the cars just seemed to sail right on by, but after a few minutes a car turned to the right and headed towards Spunky.

Grabbing another garage sale sign, Spunky thrust it above her head and waved it. The car stopped. A man and woman got out.

Spunky watched the couple cross the street and as they got close to the sidewalk she called out, "We've got a great sale here. Lots of good bargains."

"Looks very interesting," said a lady, who stopped at the far table. She picked up a vase.

Spunky held her breath. Maybe the lady would buy it. But after a few seconds, she placed it back on the table and moved on. Spunky let out a disappointed sigh.

The lady stopped at the second table. "Oh, Harold," she exclaimed in a high voice. "Come and see these adorable salt and pepper shakers."

"What have you found this time that you can't live without?" The man laughed.

"Really, Harold, these are Delft. They're quite lovely."

Spunky watched the man and woman examine the two little blue and white windmill shakers.

"See, the sails actually move around," said the woman.

"Well, I guess we better buy them before anyone else spots these little treasures." The man pulled some bills out of his pocket and handed them to Spunky.

Spunky counted the money and pushed it into the pocket of her apron. "Thanks. Would you like a bag?"

The woman nodded.

Just as she finished handing the parcel to the couple another car drove up and out popped a man. "Got any good bargains?" he asked, as he approached the table.

"All kinds," replied Spunky.

"I'll just take a quick look and see if anything interests me."

The man stopped at the middle table and stared at the creamy-white bookends. Then he lifted one of them and seemed to be weighing it in his hand. "These are nice, very nice and heavy. Onyx, I think. They'd hold my books firmly in place."

He turned the bookend around and looked at the price tag. "Seems reasonable." He reached into his pocket and pulled out some bills.

At that moment, two other cars pulled up and more people piled out and gathered around the tables. The man with the bookends reached across to hand Spunky the money. Just as Spunky was about to take it from him a high-pitched scream shattered the air.

"Stop, thief."

Chapter Fourteen

Waving her arms, Mrs. Snodgrass charged down the street. "Stop her. She's a thief." The old lady pointed at Spunky and rushed towards the tables.

People backed away and headed for their cars.

Open-mouthed, Spunky gaped at the old woman as she snatched the bookends from the man. "These are mine."

The man edged backwards and put up his hand.

"Pardon me ma'am, but I was buying them from this young lady. I thought they were hers." He motioned to Spunky and at the same time picked up his dollar bills from the table.

Spunky felt like ducking and crawling under the table as everyone turned and stared. "They are…"

"Mine." Mrs. Snodgrass barged in, pointing an accusing finger. "How dare you steal from me?"

"I didn't steal…"

"Yes, you did," said Mrs. Snodgrass, her lips quivering.

"Stolen merchandise," someone muttered.

"You can't be too careful," said another person.

"I was almost going to buy something." A lady quickly placed a floral plate back on the table.

Spunky trembled, hating the ugly word. She wasn't a thief.

"I didn't steal it," she tried to explain to the group of people who were now making their way back to their cars. Doors slammed and engines roared as people hurried to leave.

"I always thought you were a noisy little girl, but I never knew you were a thief." Mrs. Snodgrass shook her finger under Spunky's nose.

Spunky clenched her fists tight, attempting to ignore the accusations.

The few remaining people who were standing near the tables nodded their heads as if in agreement with Mrs. Snodgrass.

A voice cut through the crowd. "What's the problem?"

Spunky looked up to see her mother approaching. She walked right over to Mrs. Snodgrass and stopped beside her. "Did I hear you say the word, thief?"

"Yes," snapped Mrs. Snodgrass. "Your daughter's been selling my things. How dare she do that and where did she find them? She stole them from me."

"You're mistaken; my daughter did not steal these items. She found them in the garage."

Spunky stood a little taller. She swallowed the lump in her throat. It was nice to have her mother here sticking up for her.

For a moment Mrs. Snodgrass seemed puzzled and she didn't say anything. Then she pointed to the vase, the fancy wooden box, and the other ornaments. "These are all mine." She gave a wide sweep with her arm. "How dare you give her permission to sell them?"

"Well, I did ask Mr. Hansen, and he said they'd probably been left by a former tenant."

"Former tenant!" screeched Mrs. Snodgrass, her lips going white. "I still live in the basement. Has he forgotten how many years I've been here and faithfully paid my rent?"

"I'm sure he hasn't."

"Fifteen long years to be exact. The landlord will most certainly hear about this theft."

"I think there's been a big misunderstanding and we're sorry," Mrs. Crawford replied. "We didn't know they were yours. Please collect whatever belongs to you."

"That child of yours went through all my precious possessions."

Spunky glared at the old woman's back as Mrs. Snodgrass checked the tables, picking up cups and saucers.

"Here, let me help you with that." Mrs. Crawford took some of the china plates from the huge pile that Mrs. Snodgrass had stacked in her arms.

"You and Sammy can stay and watch the tables until I come back out."

Spunky watched her mom follow Mrs. Snodgrass across the lawn. Spunky faced Main Street and waved at Sammy. He'd left his post and was coming towards her with the mask in his hands. She slumped on the grass in the shade and rubbed her eyes with the back of her hand.

The last car drove away.

Sammy sat beside her. He looked puzzled. "I heard noise. What happened?"

"Mrs. Snodgrass accused me of stealing and now I don't know what's going to happen." Spunky twisted her hands together. She's going to call the landlord and he'll ask us to leave." Her hands shook. "We'll have no place to live."

Sammy wound the hair on the gorilla head around his finger.

"What am I going to do?" She hoped Sammy, with his logical thinking, might have an answer, but all he did was shake his head.

"I don't know."

"Snodgrass wrecked everything. It was all so perfect. I don't understand why she'd leave all those boxes in the attic if she was so fond of everything in them. It doesn't make sense."

"It almost seemed like she'd hidden them," commented Sammy.

"She likes hiding things," added Spunky, as she remembered the money Mrs. Snodgrass had stashed in the book. "She's really crazy."

"No, I don't think she is. Just a bit eccentric."

"Why don't you go home?" She bit her lips together, wanting to be alone.

"Well...if that's what you want."

"No...but..." Spunky waved her arms. "I just..." She felt discouraged and upset.

Sammy stood up. "I think my mom wants me to do some errands."

"Right." Spunky pulled her knees up to her chest and pressed her face against her arms. Why'd she say that to Sammy? All he was trying to do was help. He was her best friend and now she'd sent him away. She sniffed and wiped her nose, determined not to cry.

In a few minutes her mom returned. "You can take these downstairs. Careful, they're heavy." Her mom handed her the two horse-head bookends.

"Mrs. Snodgrass won't want to see me. Do I have to go down there?"

"Yes you do."

Spunky knew her mom was right. Maybe if she apologized, Mrs. Snodgrass wouldn't phone the landlord and they wouldn't have to move. Hoping her apology would be accepted, she collected the bookends. They felt smooth and cold and their color reminded Spunky of butterscotch-ripple ice cream. She hugged them to her chest and marched across the grass to the back door.

Inside Mrs. Snodgrass' suite she stood in the kitchen, wondering where to put the bookends.

"Don't stand there gawking."

Spunky jumped. The old grouch was right behind her, like a barking dog.

"Put them on the bookcase in the living room."

"I will." Spunky trudged into the other room and placed the items on the shelf, right beside the book. Was the money still hidden?

As she climbed the stairs, Mrs. Snodgrass was on her heals and breathing down her neck. Once she was outside, Spunky stopped and waited while Mrs. Snodgrass peered at one table and then another, her face puckered and her upper lip twisted.

Spunky wiped her wet palms on her jeans.

"Where's my carousel? You didn't sell it. Did you?" Mrs. Snodgrass scowled.

"Uh," Spunky cleared her throat. "Your carousel?"

"Yes, it had six china horses with a red and white canopy covering them. Just like you'd see in a real park."

"Um...I've got it in my room," Spunky murmured.

"Oh," gasped Mrs. Snodgrass, covering her mouth with her hand. For a second she looked really sad, but then she pulled her lips into a thin line. "That carousel is precious."

Then why'd you hide it in the garage? That question would only cause another argument, so Spunky didn't say a word. She was in enough trouble already.

Chapter Fifteen

Keeping with her promise to clean the garage, Spunky, along with help from Sammy, swept the garage floor after school.

As she pushed the broom across the floor, she thought about the money she'd made from the sale of the salt and pepper. The old lady hadn't noticed they were missing, but keeping the money wouldn't be right and she hadn't returned the carousel yet. She'd have to do that soon.

"After you left on Saturday I had to take everything down to the old grouch's suite," Spunky complained.

"What's it like?" Sammy gathered dust and pieces of paper into a pile and swept them into the pan.

"She had me running up and down the stairs so much I didn't have time to see a lot, but there's stuff all over. My mom calls it wall-to-wall furniture."

Sammy laughed. "A little crowded."

"It sure is."

Spunky pushed the last bit of dirt towards Sammy's dust pan and said, "Will you pick up this pile Sammy?"

"Okay."

Spunky leaned on the broom and gazed out the window. "Sammy," she whispered. "Look who I see." She stretched to get a better look. "Mrs. Snodgrass. She's leaving."

"Who'd you say was leaving?" asked Sammy.

"Sammy, you haven't been listening to anything I've been saying."

"I've been cleaning."

"I know. Come over here and look at her."

As Mrs. Snodgrass disappeared past the garage, Spunky laughed. "You should see the way she clutches her purse. You'd think there was a treasure inside it."

"Maybe she's got a lot of money in it."

Spunky nodded and remembered Mrs. Snodgrass counting out her money. She grabbed Sammy's arm. "I've got something to tell you."

"Go ahead."

Spunky wanted to share her great spying discovery, but she wouldn't tell Sammy right away. "It's a secret and I'm not going to tell you. I'm going to do way better. I'll show you and she'll never know."

"When are you going to start making sense?"

"Just come with me." Spunky waved her hand towards the door. "We're going to see Mrs. Snodgrass' suite."

Sammy stopped. "You can't do that. That's trespassing or...or something like that."

"Don't be silly. We're not going into her suite but we'll see it."

"What do you do? Look through the windows."

"No. Something way better. Now let's go."

Sammy hesitated. "I don't know about this."

She grabbed his hand, leading him out of the garage. When they were in the basement she proudly showed him the two furnaces. "See these."

Sammy rolled his eyes. "Oh, very interesting."

"Don't be sarcastic. It's what's behind them."

"Yeah, a wall. You think that's exciting?"

"If you'll keep quiet for a minute I'll show you." Spunky squeezed into the space between the furnace and the wall.

Now she couldn't see Sammy so she poked her head out. "See, I can hide behind here."

"Oh, I get it; you've found a new place to play hide-and-go-seek."

"No, stupid, follow me."

Sammy edged into the space. "Two squashed bodies instead of one."

She inched her way past the second furnace with Sammy close behind. "We're here. This is it."

Sammy gawked around. "What's so great about being in a little closet?"

"Look at these slats? You can see through them and right into her suite." Spunky pressed her nose against the door and surveyed the suite. "You look now." She backed away and Sammy peered through the slats.

"She sure has lots of stuff."

"Look to your right. Do you see all the toys on her bed?"

"Wow, she must really like them."

Thump. Thump.

Sammy backed away from the door, "What's that?" he whispered.

"Someone's coming down the stairs." Spunky kept her voice low.

The noise on the stairs got louder and Spunky heard a man's voice. Her heart hammered against her chest. Why had she decided to bring Sammy to the basement? She'd get both of them in trouble. What would her mom think? She'd let her mom down again.

"We'd better get out of here," said Sammy.

She grabbed his sleeve. "They'll see us. Mrs. Snodgrass must have company. We'll sneak out as soon as they get into the suite."

The door rattled.

"I won't give it to you," squeaked the old lady.

Spunky frowned. What did Mrs. Snodgrass mean? Peering through the door, she strained to see what was happening. Mrs. Snodgrass came into the living room and beside her was a man. He had long scraggly hair and Spunky noticed that he hadn't shaved.

"I don't have any money," said Mrs. Snodgrass.

"Quit stalling." The man pulled his upper lip. "I know you've got some stashed down here and you'll be very sorry if you don't give it to me."

Spunky caught her breath. This man wasn't a friend. He was going to rob Mrs. Snodgrass. They had to get help.

Frantically, Spunky signaled for Sammy to leave and call the police.

"I told you, I don't have any money," protested Mrs. Snodgrass.

"Oh yes you do. I know you go to the bank and get money."

"I didn't this week."

"Don't lie to me. I've been watching you. I want the money now."

Spunky's heart felt like it was in her throat. What could she do? Had Sammy got to a phone?

"You're wrong," said Mrs. Snodgrass.

"Quit the stalling and tell me now old lady. Where is it?" He twisted her arm.

"You're hurting me." Mrs. Snodgrass' face went white and Spunky winced.

"I'll give you one last chance."

Where was Sammy? Mrs. Snodgrass needed help, and if the police didn't come soon she'd be hurt.

"Ouch, let go of my arm."

Spunky cringed as the old woman whimpered and stumbled forward.

"Just as soon as you show me where the money is."

She had to help Mrs. Snodgrass, but how?

"It's...it's...over here." Mrs. Snodgrass motioned with her head towards the bookcase.

"Show me." Facing the opposite direction, the man had his back to Spunky.

She searched round the darkened closet. What could she do? She spied the baseball bat. It was sticking out of the box, where it had fallen over on the floor. Her hands shook as she grabbed the bat. She kicked the door open and charged towards the burglar, swinging the bat and smashing the man on the back of the knees. Thwack!

"Ow!" howled the burglar.

He loosened his grip on Mrs. Snodgrass and Spunky gave him another sharp crack. This time his knees buckled, but he caught himself and turned on Spunky, his face twisting into a threatening scowl. He reached out to grab her, but she jumped away, just in time.

"You little...."

He snarled, but didn't have time to say any more because Mrs. Snodgrass smacked him on the shoulder with the horse-head bookend.

"What the..." He stumbled towards the kitchen.

"Get him," yelled Mrs. Snodgrass.

Spunky took another swing, but the man was out of her reach.

"Don't let him get away," hollered Mrs. Snodgrass.

The man scrambled out through the kitchen and up the stairs, all the time putting more distance between himself and Spunky.

"We've lost him." Mrs. Snodgrass stopped at the top of the stairs and took a big gulp of air.

"I'll catch him," Spunky yelled over her shoulder. She raced out the back door and down the steps. By the time she reached the front street, the robber had disappeared.

Chapter Sixteen

The whine of a siren announced the arrival of the police.

Waving her arms, Spunky ran towards the police car. It stopped. "He's getting away."

The officer stepped out of the car. Mrs. Snodgrass grabbed his arm. "The thief. You've got to catch him Adam."

He patted Mrs. Snodgrass' hand and Spunky noticed his kind dark eyes as he smiled.

"Oh, Adam. That horrible man tried to rob me and you're letting him get away."

"Everything's going to be okay, thanks to this young man." Officer Adam pointed to the back seat of the car.

Spunky squinted and peered through the window. "Sammy," she cried. "I didn't see you."

"I know," replied Sammy, the grin on his face getting bigger.

"How'd you get the cops here?"

"I called 911."

"Wow," exclaimed Spunky. "That's great." Another police car drove up.

"That's him." Mrs. Snodgrass was shaking, as she pointed to the other car. "That's the thief in the sheriff's car."

"I assume we have the man who was trying to rob you then." There was a twinkle of satisfaction in Deputy Thorley's eyes.

"Yes, yes." Mrs. Snodgrass jumped up and down.

Spunky smiled. The old woman looked kind of crazy. No, not crazy, just funny and happy.

"She did it." Mrs. Snodgrass pointed her finger at Spunky.

Spunky backed away. "What did I do wrong now?"

"She did what?" asked the deputy.

"She saved me. That's what she did."

The deputy turned his attention to Spunky. "What did you do?"

Mrs. Snodgrass didn't give Spunky a chance to reply. "She clobbered him. You should have seen her. Boy, did we give that robber a run for his money."

Spunky couldn't help grinning. "That's the first nice thing she's ever said about me," she whispered to Sammy, who was now standing on the sidewalk beside her.

"Sounds like she thinks you're okay."

Spunky's tone was still uncertain. "Maybe. We'll see." She was still worried that Mrs. Snodgrass had reported her to the landlord.

The sheriff drove away with the thief.

"We've had our eye on this guy for a while. He's a drifter, recently in town," explained Deputy Thorley.

After getting their stories, the deputy drove away. Without a word to Spunky, Mrs. Snodgrass held her head high and marched into the house.

***

Feeling down in the dumps Spunky went into the house. Just as she stepped into the house, the phone rang. She picked up the receiver.

"Hello."

"Hello, may I please speak to Mrs. Crawford?" said a man.

"She's busy right now. Could I take a message?" Unless she knew the caller, Spunky never let them know her mother wasn't home.

"Yes, thank you. Please tell her that Mr. Hansen called, and he'll be over tonight."

"Okay." The sound caught in her throat. "I'll tell her." Slowly she placed the phone back.

Mrs. Snodgrass had phoned and complained about the garage sale. Spunky's heart pounded as she raced down the hall and collapsed against the pillows on her bed.

Mean old Mr. Hansen was coming over tonight to evict them. Her mom had said that she was supposed to be nice to Mrs. Snodgrass and even though she'd saved the old lady, she'd still reported Spunky for the garage items.

She and her mom were going to be kicked out of the house and there was nothing she could do.

Chapter Seventeen

Later that night, Spunky sat frozen in the living room chair as she watched her mom straighten her skirt and glance in the mirror before she opened the front door.

"Good evening, Mr. Hansen," said Mrs. Crawford. Spunky noticed the polite, but nervous smile on her mom's face.

"Hello, Mrs. Crawford." The landlord sounded pleasant and he smiled, but Spunky knew why he was here.

"Please come in." Mrs. Crawford stepped back, allowing the landlord to enter the living room.

He nodded his head. "Thank you. It's such a pleasant evening to be out."

"Oh, yes, I so love this time of year with the gold and red leaves."

She's not going to love it when she finds out what's going to happen, thought Spunky.

"Mr. Hansen, I'd like you to meet my daughter, Sarah."

There it was again. Her mom only called her Sarah when she was in trouble.

"Sarah," her mother's tone sounded sharper.

Spunky slowly looked up. Mr. Hansen was standing right in front of her and he was holding his hand out. He didn't have white hair like she thought he would. His hair was brown and he looked like he was her mom's age.

"Sarah," her mother prompted.

Remembering her manners, Spunky stood and put her hand out to Mr. Hansen. It seemed to get lost in his.

Mr. Hansen pumped her hand. "Nice to meet you."

Once again Spunky stared at him. He was smiling at her and his blue eyes seemed to twinkle. She gulped, and for a second she thought of someone else, but she couldn't remember who. "Hi," was all she could manage to say.

"Won't you have a seat, Mr. Hansen?"

"Thank you." He sat down and gazed at Spunky's mom. "Please call me Jack."

Mrs. Crawford blushed.

Mr. Hansen turned to Spunky. "I hear you did something special today."

Spunky nodded, not saying a word.

"I think, and so do the police, that what you did was very brave. I've heard a glowing report from Deputy Adam. He said you saved Mrs. Snodgrass. Your mother must be very proud of you."

Spunky bowed her head. "I hope so."

"I am." Her mom beamed, making Spunky feel a little better. "I hear Sarah clobbered the intruder with a baseball bat. I can't imagine why Mrs. Snodgrass had such a thing in her closet, but it's a good thing that she did."

"Those were probably mine. Were they a light brown color?" asked Mr. Hansen.

Instead of answering, Spunky bobbed her head.

Mr. Hansen laughed. "Your daughter's very quiet. Not like most kids I've known."

"Well I must say that this is the first time I've ever seen Sarah at a loss for words."

Spunky glared at her mother.

"Could I get you a cup of coffee?" asked Mrs. Crawford

"Sounds good," replied Mr. Hansen.

She got up and left the room. Now Spunky was alone with the landlord. She stared at the floor, and then gradually met his gaze.

In a friendly voice he asked, "How do you like it here?"

"Fine." She didn't have much to say to a man who'd evict them.

"When your mother said she had a daughter, I thought this would be a nice place for a child. Lots of room in the yard for outdoor sports."

"It would if we weren't being evicted," blurted Spunky.

Mr. Hansen opened his mouth to speak, but Spunky didn't let him start. "If it weren't for horrible old Mrs. Snodgrass we could stay here."

Mr. Hansen looked puzzled. "I think I missed something. What has Mrs. Snodgrass got to do with you being evicted?"

"Well, didn't she phone you and complain about me?"

Mr. Hansen seemed confused. "If she did, I didn't hear anything about it."

Now Spunky really felt upset, and puzzled. "Didn't she complain about how I stole her stuff, and tried to sell it?"

Mrs. Crawford entered the room carrying a tray with two cups and cream and sugar. She set it down on the table in front of Mr. Hansen.

He picked up the coffee cup. "I'm baffled about what's been happening."

"Do you remember those items that were boxed in the garage?" Spunky's mom asked.

"Yes, I said you could sell them because I'd left them there and I didn't think I'd ever use them. I'd always meant to sell them or give them away to some charity."

"Apparently, there were some boxes that belonged to Mrs. Snodgrass. I don't understand why she hid them in the attic. They seemed to be valuable," Spunky's mom explained.

Mr. Hansen nodded. "I think I might be able to shed some light on your question. One day when I had tea with her she seemed to be really 'down' and I asked her why. She told me that she was thinking about her daughter. She only had one child and it would have been her birthday, but Maria died when she was twelve."

"That's terrible," said Mrs. Crawford. "No wonder she was so angry."

"After I knew about Maria, I tried to be understanding when Mrs. Snodgrass was short-tempered and complained. I should have explained about her loss, but you seemed so anxious and pleased to live here, I didn't mention it. I thought you and your daughter would enjoy this house and the yard."

"I do. We do." Spunky's mom put her hand over her mouth.

"I've often thought Mrs. Snodgrass is still bitter about the loss."

"The poor woman," said Mrs. Crawford. "No wonder she was so annoyed when she found Spunky selling her treasures."

"And now you're going to evict us because she complained to you." Spunky huddled in the chair.

"Who said that?" asked Mr. Hansen.

Spunky stammered, "Well... I... my mom said..."

Her mom cut in, "I'm afraid it's my fault. I've told Sarah that she must get along with Mrs. Snodgrass and that it's important for us to remain living here. If we couldn't get along with her, we might be evicted."

Mr. Hansen's eyes opened wide, like Sammy's, when he was surprised. "I've no intention of doing that." He turned to Spunky. "You really thought I'd evict you and your mother?"

Under his close scrutiny, Spunky felt kind of silly. She chewed on her finger. "Yes," she said, not wanting to look straight at him.

"Kids." Mr. Hansen laughed. "They have such wonderful imaginations."

This wasn't fair. He was laughing at her. "Then why are you here?" she demanded.

"Sarah, what's today's date?" asked her mom.

Why was her mother asking her the date? She shrugged. "I don't know."

"It's the first of the month."

"So? I know that."

"On the first of the month the rent is due and Mr. Hansen was kind enough to drop around to collect it, because in all the excitement I'd forgotten to mail him a check."

"Oh," said Spunky. She turned to Mr. Hansen. "You're not kicking us out?"

He grinned. "Sarah Crawford, that thought never crossed my mind."

"But what about Mrs. Snodgrass?" questioned Spunky. "Hasn't she phoned you about me and told you all the things I've done wrong?"

"Don't worry. Mrs. Snodgrass is a good tenant, but between you and me she can be a bit cranky at times." He winked at Spunky.

"Then you're not mad at us?"

"No, I'm not, Sarah."

"Good, that's a relief." Spunky sat up straight. "I was sure she'd squeal on me and I was so worried. I'm really sorry about her daughter."

"You had no way of knowing, and it was an honest mistake. Now might be a good time for you to start off on the right foot," continued Mr. Hansen.

"Yes, I think it's a good idea, Jack." Mrs. Crawford turned to Spunky. "Why don't you go downstairs and see her now."

"Won't you come with me? Please, Mom?"

"No, it might not be as bad as you think."

Spunky bit her lips together. She'd been meaning to return the carousel but she hadn't and she didn't want to face the old lady again. "Mom, I have something of hers."

Her mother frowned. "What?"

"I found a carousel in the garage."

"Then what should you do?"

Spunky sighed, "Take it back." She dragged herself into the bedroom and lifted the carousel from the dresser. After plodding, at a snail's pace, she finally reached the basement.

Chapter Eighteen

Spunky knocked twice and waited. If she was lucky Mrs. Snodgrass wouldn't be home.

From behind the door squeaked the all too familiar voice, "Coming."

"Drat," muttered Spunky. After hiding in the closet and then whacking the thief, she wasn't sure what she'd say. Would Mrs. Snodgrass be pleased or annoyed to see her?

The door opened a crack and Mrs. Snodgrass peeked out.

Spunky stared silently into a pair of pale brown eyes. Mrs. Snodgrass wasn't smiling and her lips were firmly pressed together. For several seconds she didn't say anything. She opened the door wider and reached out. Reluctantly, Spunky handed the carousel to her.

"Come in."

Half-heartedly Spunky stepped into the kitchen. Feeling shy, she stood with her hands clasped and looked around. Bowls and cookie trays were scattered on the counter. The room was warm, and it smelled like peanut butter cookies.

Mrs. Snodgrass was so busy examining the carousel that she seemed to have forgotten Spunky. The old lady ran her finger over the back of one of the black horses. She removed her glasses, squinted and leaned closer to the horse. "You've been playing with the music box, haven't you?"

Spunky held her breath, hoping the old lady wouldn't accuse her of wrecking it.

Mrs. Snodgrass continued, "You know, this belonged to a very special little girl."

"Maria?" asked Spunky.

Mrs. Snodgrass lifted the corner of her apron and wiped under her glasses. "Yes."

"I'm sorry," murmured Spunky, and suddenly she felt bad for all the awful things she had thought and said about Mrs. Snodgrass.

"Maria loved to play it at night, just before she went to bed." The old lady lifted the carousel and handed it to Spunky. She coughed and cleared her throat. "I know you love it, and now it should go to another young person who will enjoy it."

"I...I...," stuttered Spunky.

"Ssh." Mrs. Snodgrass pressed her finger to her lip and blinked. "Say no more. It's time for me to let the bitter memories go."

"Thank you. I love this carousel and I'll take good care of it." She walked towards the door.

"You can tell your mother that I'd like her and Jack to come down here and see me. You come too."

Spunky turned and smiled at the old lady. "Okay".

"I mean in the next five minutes."

Spunky sighed. It didn't look like all her troubles were over yet. Why did Mrs. Snodgrass want to see all of them at once, and why had she given her the carousel, if she still was mad?

Back in her bedroom Spunky placed the carousel on the dresser, and then she trudged into the living room. Mr. Hansen and her mom were deep in conversation.

Her mother raised her head, "How did it go with Mrs. Snodgrass?"

"She gave me the carousel."

"That's wonderful." Her mom's face glowed. "Oh, Jack, I think things are looking better."

Spunky shook her head, distressed that her mom might be in for a big surprise. "Mom, I don't know about that. Mrs. Snodgrass wants to see all of us. *Now!* That's what she said!"

Mr. Hansen laughed. "Sounds ominous. I wonder what she's up to. Let's find out."

When they reached the bottom of the stairs, Mr. Hansen knocked on the door.

Mrs. Snodgrass opened it and waved her hand. "Come in, come in. Let's sit in the living room." She led the way.

Spunky dropped onto the sofa and her mother sat beside her. Across from them sat Mr. Hansen in one chair, and Mrs. Snodgrass in the other.

"How could you give permission for a little girl to sell my valuable possessions?" Mrs. Snodgrass accused Mr. Hansen.

His face reddened. "I thought it was just my old junk in there that I'd never gotten around to giving away or trying to sell. How was I to know that you'd decided to store your beautiful china and ornaments in the garage attic?"

"Well, well." Mrs. Snodgrass paused, seeming at a loss for words.

The lines in her face didn't seem so deep and Spunky hastened to add, "I really wasn't stealing from you. I'd never do that."

Mrs. Snodgrass bowed her head. "I understand that now."

"No harm done," said Mr. Hansen. His cheery voice filled the room.

"And you, young lady." Mrs. Snodgrass indicated Spunky. "You are to be congratulated for helping me this afternoon."

"That's okay. I didn't want him to hurt you. Besides, it was kind of fun."

Mrs. Snodgrass raised her fist. "We sure scared the living daylights out of him. Did you see the way he ran up the stairs? He was a coward."

"You're right," agreed Spunky. "He tried to pick on you just because you're old."

"Ha," said Mrs. Snodgrass. "He got more than he bargained for. Teach him not to mess with us." She winked at Spunky.

For the first time Spunky saw Mrs. Snodgrass smile. It was a friendly smile, and Spunky thought she looked a lot nicer.

Mrs. Snodgrass abruptly stood. "How about some cookies?" She went to the kitchen and quickly returned with a loaded plate of goodies, offering them first to Mr. Hansen.

Mrs. Snodgrass waited as he chomped into one. "These are as tasty as I remember them. You still make the best peanut butter cookies I've ever had."

"If you'd come around here more often, Jack Hansen, I'd give you some."

Mr. Hansen laughed and gazed at Spunky's mom. "I think I might."

Mrs. Crawford's face turned red.

He looked at Spunky. "Everything seems to have worked out fine for you now that you have the carousel, and you know I'm not going to evict you and your mom."

"Oh, yes," replied Spunky. "But I still didn't make any money for my new bike."

"So the garage sale was a way for you to earn money? Right?" asked Mr. Hansen.

Spunky nodded.

"Are you still interested in some sort of money making project?"

"Oh yes, but, how?"

"Not selling other peoples' things, I hope," said Mrs. Snodgrass.

"Oh, no," exclaimed Spunky. "I'm really sorry about that."

"I know, child, I was just joking."

"I think I just might have a plan." Mr. Hansen rubbed his chin and appeared to be considering carefully. "I could do with a helper, if that's okay with your mother."

"Would you let Sarah help me with the gardening when I come over to cut the lawn every week? She could cultivate the flower beds, pull weeds and do other odd jobs."

"Sounds fine to me," said her mom.

"How does that sound to you, Sarah?" he asked.

Spunky jumped up. "Can my friend, Sammy, help too?"

"I don't see why not. Is he a good worker?"

"Oh, yes. He's great," answered Spunky.

"Then the two of you can share the money that I pay you."

"Wow, I'll tell him at school, on Monday."

Mr. Hansen stood up and shook Spunky's hand. "Looks like we've got a deal, Sarah."

Spunky stood as tall as she could. "Right," she answered solemnly.

She looked at Mrs. Snodgrass and back at Mr. Hansen. "And my name isn't Sarah. My friends call me Spunky."

"Spunky!" snorted Mrs. Snodgrass and Mr. Hansen chuckled.

"Spunky." They both laughed. "The name fits."

CPSIA information can be obtained at www.ICGtesting.com
Printed in the USA
LVOW09s0823030914

402085LV00001B/16/P